PETER HADDOCK PUBLISHING

Published by
Peter Haddock Publishing,
United Kingdom YO16 6BT

Bedtime Stories

CONTENTS

This Book Belongs to

Ben. morrison. 114 Glen rode.

The House That Jack Built

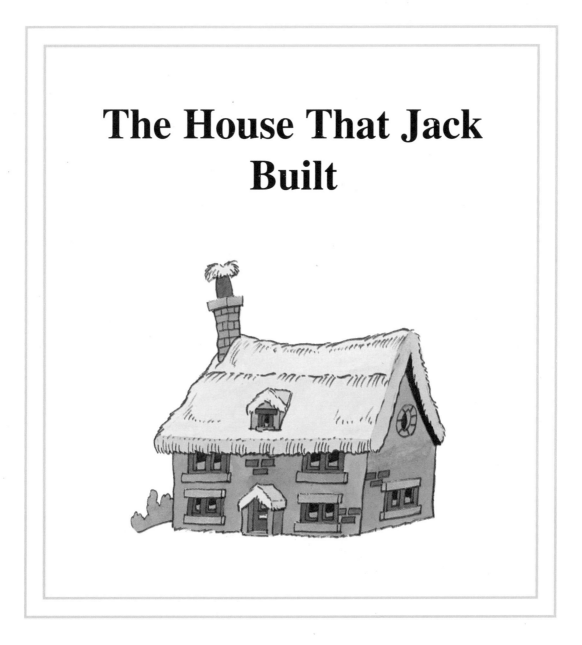

The House That Jack Built

This is the house that Jack built.

This is the malt,
That lay in the house that Jack built.

This is the rat,
That ate the malt,
That lay in the house that Jack built.

This is the cat,
That killed the rat,
That ate the malt,
That lay in the house that Jack built.

This is the dog,
That worried the cat,
That killed the rat,
That ate the malt,
That lay in the house that Jack built.

This is the cow with the crumpled horn,
That tossed the dog,
That worried the cat,
That killed the rat,
That ate the malt,
That lay in the house that Jack built.

This is the maiden all forlorn,
That milked the cow with the crumpled horn,
That tossed the dog,
That worried the cat,
That killed the rat,
That ate the malt,
That lay in the house that Jack built.

This is the man all tattered and torn,

That kissed the maiden all forlorn,

That milked the cow with the crumpled horn,

That tossed the dog,

That worried the cat,

That killed the rat,

That ate the malt,

That lay in the house that Jack built.

This is the priest all shaven and shorn,

That married the man all tattered and torn,

That kissed the maiden all forlorn,

That milked the cow with the crumpled horn,

That tossed the dog,
That worried the cat,
That killed the rat,
That ate the malt,
That lay in the house that Jack built.

This is the cock that crowed in the morn,
That woke the priest all shaven and shorn,
That married the man all tattered and torn,
That kissed the maiden all forlorn,
That milked the cow with the crumpled horn,

That tossed the dog,
That worried the cat,
That killed the rat,
That ate the malt,
That lay in the house that Jack built.

This is the farmer that sowed the corn,
That fed the cock that crowed in the morn,
That woke the priest all shaven and shorn,
That married the man all tattered and torn,
That kissed the maiden all forlorn,
That milked the cow with the crumpled horn,

That tossed the dog,
That worried the cat,
That killed the rat,
That ate the malt,
That lay in the house that Jack built.

That was the house that Jack built.

The Three Billy Goats Gruff

The Three Billy Goats Gruff

Once upon a time there were three billy goats who lived in a field. They were known as the Billy Goats Gruff and they were brothers.

The oldest brother was very big and fierce-looking with a big, bushy beard and long, curling horns. The middle-sized brother was smaller and looked more gentle. He had a soft, wavy beard and shorter horns. The youngest brother was very small and looked timid. His horns were short and he had hardly any beard at all.

The Billy Goats Gruff were happy munching away at the grass in the field. However, after a while the grass began to look bare and thin.

Now, over the river there was a bigger field full of the greenest grass that the Billy Goats Gruff had ever seen. The river was fast and deep and the only way to get to the other side was over a rickety, wooden bridge but, under the bridge, lived a fearsome ugly troll who would jump out and gobble up anybody who tried to cross over.

The grass in the goats' field grew thinner and thinner and one day the eldest Billy Goat Gruff called his brothers to him and said,

"If we stay here much longer we will starve. We must try to cross the bridge but how can we get past that ugly troll?"

The other two thought for a moment and then the youngest goat said,

"I have a plan. Listen to me..."

A few moments later, the youngest Billy Goat Gruff trotted bravely up and, taking a deep breath, he stepped lightly on to the bridge.

'Trip-trap, trip-trap' went his hooves on the rickety wood. The troll jumped out.

"Who goes trip-trapping on my bridge?"

"Only the youngest Billy Goat Gruff," squeaked the little goat.

"Goody-goody. I'm going to gobble you up!" growled the troll.

"Wait, Mr Troll. Look how small I am. My big brother will be coming in a minute. He's much fatter. Why spoil your appetite?"

The troll grumbled and groaned and then said,

"Very well, off you go! Your brother will make a much tastier meal. I shall wait for him."

The youngest Billy Goat Gruff tripped and trapped over the bridge and the troll climbed back down to his hiding place to wait.

A few moments later the middle-sized Billy Goat Gruff trotted bravely up and stepped firmly on to the bridge. 'TRIP-TRAP, TRIP-TRAP' went his hooves on the rickety wood.

Out jumped the troll, angrier than before.

"Who goes trip-trapping on my bridge?"

"Only the middle-sized Billy Goat Gruff," replied the middle-sized goat calmly.

"Goody-goody! I've been waiting for you! I'm going to gobble you up," gloated the troll.

"Wait, Mr Troll. My big brother, who is coming soon is much bigger than I am. Why spoil your appetite?"

Once more the troll grumbled and then said,

"All right. Off you go! Your big brother will make an even tastier meal. I shall wait for him!"

The middle-sized Billy Goat Gruff tripped and trapped over the bridge. The troll climbed back to his hiding place and a few moments later the eldest Billy Goat Gruff trotted bravely along.

Taking a deep breath, he stamped loudly on the the bridge. **'TRIP-TRAP, TRIP-TRAP'** went his hooves on the rickety wood. The troll jumped out, angrier and uglier than ever.

"Who goes trip-trapping on my bridge?"

"I am the eldest Billy Goat Gruff," announced the big goat proudly.

"Goody-goody! So YOU are the one I've been waiting for. I'm going to gobble you up!"

"Oh no, Mr Troll, I don't think so!" The eldest Billy Goat Gruff tossed his horns in defiance, then stood up straight and tall and looked the fierce troll right in the eye. "I am going to cross the bridge!" he said in his fierce, deep voice.

The troll took a step forward.

'THUMP, THUMP THUMP!' went the front hooves of the eldest Billy Goat Gruff as he scraped them on the bridge in anger.

The troll took another step.

All of a sudden, the eldest Billy Goat Gruff charged at the fierce, ugly troll. He butted him with his long, curling horns as hard as he could.

'BOOMPH!' The troll flew through the air.

'SPLASH!' He landed in the river and was swept right away downstream, never to be seen again.

The eldest Billy Goat Gruff tripped and trapped proudly over the bridge to join his two younger brothers.

There on the other side of the deep river they had all the finest green grass they could eat and the three Billy Goats Gruff never ran out of grass again.

When people heard that the big, ugly troll was no more, they began to use the bridge again and, every time they crossed over, they would always wave a grateful 'Thank you' to the three Billy Goats Gruff.

The Hare and The Tortoise

The Hare and The Tortoise

It was a lovely, sunny day, but the animals in the forest were paying no attention to the weather. They were arguing about which of them could run the fastest. Hare, as usual, was boasting.

"I am the fastest by far! I will race any of you. The prize will be this gold button. Squirrel, how about you?"

"No fear, Hare, not I," giggled Squirrel.

"Fox, do you want to race me?"

Fox shook his head silently.

"Is nobody brave enough to try to beat me in a race? Badger? Hedgehog? Weasel? . . . Nobody?"

There was silence for a minute or two and then a tiny voice said,

"I'll have a try, if you like."

Hare turned round and saw Tortoise plodding slowly across the field at the edge of the forest.

Hare giggled quietly to himself and tried to keep his face straight as he spoke to Tortoise.

"Ah, Tortoise! So you are here - at last!"

"I saw no reason to hurry," said Tortoise. "It's such a lovely day, after all."

"It seems that you are my only challenger. Are you willing to race me to the stone bridge on the other side of the wood for this fine prize?"

"It certainly is a fine prize and a race to the bridge sounds fair enough. Yes, I am willing to race you," said Tortoise slowly and carefully.

"Old Slowcoach!" laughed Hare. "You *must* be joking! You have no chance of beating me!"

The other animals joined in the laughter but Tortoise shook his head slowly.

"Indeed I am not joking!" he said. "Now, who is going to start us off?"

Hare was still laughing as the two animals lined up and waited for Owl's starting signal.

"Tu-whit-tu-whoo!"

The 'tu-whoo' had hardly left Owl's beak when Hare was off like the wind, speeding through the trees. Tortoise was still plodding into the edge of the woods when Hare was out of sight.

"Come on, Tortoise!" cheered the other animals laughing. "Can't you go faster than that?"

"I don't know why you bother," said Badger.

"Hare will win by miles," said Hedgehog.

Tortoise did not show that he was hurt by these unkind remarks. Instead, he just kept plodding on, all the time saying to himself,

"Slow and steady wins the race: slow and steady ..."

Hare charged relentlessly on through the woods. He looked back but there was no sign of Tortoise so he lolloped on more gently for a few more minutes and then stopped again. He was now at the far edge of the wood and, in front of him, he could see the old, stone bridge - the finishing post of the race.

Hare, being a bit of a show-off, did not like the idea of finishing with no-one there to cheer him so he sat down under a tree to wait until the other animals caught up. Then he would make a triumphant dash for the bridge. It was a hot day, however, and Hare had to close his eyes against the glare of the sun. In the twinkling of an eye he had dozed off to sleep.

It was late afternoon when Hare woke up and the sun was no longer fierce and hot. As he got up he caught the sound of the other animals in a state of excitement - twittering, squeaking and hooting.

"Goody!" he thought. "They're here to see me win. Poor old Tortoise. He'll be miles behind."

Hare had a little stretch and got ready to run again. He did not know, however, that, all the time he had been sleeping, Tortoise had been trudging slowly but steadily on through the woods. In fact Hare had been asleep long enough for Tortoise to catch up with him and pass him and he did not realize that the animals were cheering Tortoise and not him!

Tortoise was now only a couple of steps away from the old, stone bridge. All of a sudden, Hare caught sight of Tortoise and, with horror, realized what had happened.

He could not believe how foolish he had been. It did not matter now how hard he ran for it was too late to catch up with Tortoise and all the other animals were there to see Tortoise win.

Tortoise plodded the last step to the bridge and stood there glowing with pride. It was one of the happiest days of his life. He had beaten Hare and the other animals cheered him.

"Good old Tortoise! You've won! Well done!"

Poor Hare! How silly he felt to think of everybody watching him sleeping as Tortoise passed him! He wished he had never boasted.

"Here you are. Here's the gold button prize," he muttered, ears drooping. "And - well done!"

"You can keep the button, Hare," said Tortoise kindly. "I've had a lot of fun today. Just remember; slow and steady wins the race, slow and steady . . ."

The Frog Prince

The Frog Prince

A princess went into a wood one fine evening and sat down on the bank of a cool stream. In her hand she had a ball, which was her favourite plaything, and she amused herself by tossing it into the air and catching it again as it fell.

After a time she threw it up so high that, when she stretched out her hand to catch it, the ball bounced away along the grass until at last it rolled into the water.

The princess looked in the stream to find her ball but the water was so very deep that she could not see the bottom and she began to cry bitterly.

She sobbed and said,

"Alas! If only I could have my beautiful ball back I would give all my fine clothes, my jewels and everything I have in the world!"

As she was crying, a frog put its head out of the water and asked,

"Princess, why do you weep so bitterly?"

"My ball has rolled into the pool but how can a nasty, slimy frog like you help me?"

The frog said,

"I do not want your fine clothes and jewels but if you will let me sit at the table with you and eat from your own golden plate and sleep on your own pillow, I will bring your ball again."

"What nonsense the frog is talking," she thought. "He can never reach the palace."

Then the princess thought to herself that the frog might be able to get the ball and so she decided to agree to what he asked and said,

"Well, if you can bring me my ball I will do as you ask."

Then the frog dived deep under the water and after a little while he came up again with the ball in his mouth and tossed it to the princess.

As soon as the princess caught her ball she ran home as fast as she could and gave no more thought to the poor frog who called after her,

"Princess, stop! Take me with you as you promised."

But the princess was far away, running across the grass to the palace and clasping the precious ball.

The next day, just as the princess sat down to supper, she heard a strange noise as if something wet were climbing up the marble stairs. There was a tapping at the door and a voice cried,

"Open the door, my Princess dear,
Open the door to thy true love here!
And remember the promise thou hast made
By the river cool in the greenwood shade."

Then the princess ran and opened the door and saw the frog, whom she had quite forgotten. She was terrified and, shutting the door as fast as she could she ran back to her seat. The king, her father, asked her what had frightened her.

"There is a frog at the door," said she, "who brought my ball out of the pool. As a reward I promised that he should sit at the table with me, eat from my plate and sleep on my pillow. I thought he would never be able to reach the palace but, oh dear, here he is and he wants to come in!"

While she was speaking the frog knocked again and repeated his request.

"As you have made a promise, you must keep it," said the king sternly. "Let him in!"

She did so and the frog hopped into the room, coming close to the table and saying,

"Lift me on to a chair so I can sit next to you."

As soon as she had done so the frog said,

"Put your plate closer so I may eat from it."

When he had eaten his fill the frog said,

"Now I am tired. Carry me upstairs and let me sleep on your pillow."

So the princess took him in her hand and put him on the pillow of her own bed where he slept all night long. As soon as it was light he jumped up, hopped downstairs and left the palace.

"Now he is gone," thought the princess, "and I shall be troubled with him no more."

In this she was mistaken for, that night, she heard the same tapping at the door and the frog again sat by her, ate from her plate and then slept on her pillow all that night as well. The same happened on the third night but, when she awoke the next morning there, standing at the foot of her bed, was a handsome prince gazing down at her.

He told her that he had been enchanted by a malicious fairy who changed him into a frog, in which form he was fated to remain until a princess should let him sleep upon her bed for three nights.

"You," said the prince, "have broken this cruel enchantment and now all I wish is that you should go with me into my father's kingdom, where I will marry you and love you for as long as I live."

The king gladly bestowed his daughter's hand in marriage on the handsome prince and they were married in a splendid ceremony. The king gave them a magnificent carriage drawn by six beautiful horses with golden harness and they travelled to the prince's palace in the mountains where they lived happily ever after.

The Gingerbread Man

The Gingerbread Man

There was once an old woman who loved baking. One day, she was baking gingerbread and had enough mixture to make three big loaves with a little left over. Smiling to herself, she moulded the sticky mixture into the shape of a little man. She added currant eyes, nose and mouth and gave him four little currant buttons down his front.

"This will be a treat for my husband," she said.

When her husband came home the old woman opened the oven door and took out the loaves. Then she lifted out the gingerbread man.

"What a lovely surprise! I shall eat him after my supper," said the old man.

At these words, the gingerbread man suddenly came to life.

"Oh no, you WON'T!" he declared loudly, jumped to his feet, leapt down from the table and ran out of the door.

The old woman and the old man, astonished at this strange happening, gave chase at once but the gingerbread man was too fast for them.

"Run, run, as fast as you can!" he cried. "You can't catch me, I'm the gingerbread man!"

A dog saw the gingerbread man as he ran by.

"Mm! Very tasty," he thought and joined the chase but the gingerbread man only laughed.

On ran the gingerbread man with the old woman, the old man and the dog all chasing him.

He passed a boy kicking stones along the road and when the boy saw the gingerbread man he stopped and exclaimed,

"A gingerbread man! I would love to eat that."

So he began to chase him as well but the gingerbread man just laughed and said,

"Run, run, as fast as you can! You can't catch me, I'm the gingerbread man!"

The gingerbread man ran on and soon passed two road-menders. When they saw him, they dropped their shovels and ran after him.

"A gingerbread man! Just right for our tea."

The gingerbread man only laughed and said,

"Run, run, as fast as you can! You can't catch me, I'm the gingerbread man!"

The chase continued and soon they passed a horse, grazing in the field. The horse saw the gingerbread man and licked his lips.

"A gingerbread man would be a nice change from grass," he said, jumping over the fence, but the gingerbread man only laughed and said,

"Run, run, as fast as you can! You can't catch me, I'm the gingerbread man!"

The horse could gallop fast but not fast enough. The gingerbread man ran like the wind laughing all the time as he went along.

"Run, run!" he called out gleefully. "Run, run, as fast as you can! You can't catch me, I'm the gingerbread man!"

And those that ran after him puffed and panted more and more.

The gingerbread man began to run through the fields and still he laughed. The old woman, the old man, the dog, the boy, the road-menders and the horse still chased him but they were falling further back and could not carry on much longer.

Then, suddenly, the gingerbread man stopped. He had come to a deep and fast-flowing river too wide to jump across. There was no bridge and he could not swim. The old woman, the old man, the dog, the boy, the road-menders and the horse were still coming after him, so he could not go back.

"What shall I do?" he said to himself. "They must not catch the gingerbread man!"

At that moment, the gingerbread man heard a silky-smooth voice in his ear, saying,

"I can help you get across the river."

The gingerbread man turned and saw a fox standing beside him, smiling.

"Jump on to my back and I'll carry you across, if you like," said the fox.

"Mind you don't get me wet!" he said and then he turned to laugh at the old woman, the old man, the dog, the boy, the road-menders and the horse, who were all running towards the river-bank.

"Run, run, as fast as you can! You can't catch me, I'm the gingerbread man!"

The fox waded to the middle of the river.

"The water's getting deeper now," he told the gingerbread man. "You had better climb higher."

The gingerbread man did as he was told.

"The water is getting deeper still," warned the fox. "Climb on to my head or you will get wet!"

He climbed up and, looking back at the river-bank, where the old woman, the old man, the dog, the boy, the road-menders and the horse were standing, he called out,

"Run, run, as fast as you can! You can't catch me, I'm the gingerbread man!"

They all watched as the fox spoke again,

"It's still too deep! Climb on to the tip of my nose if you want to stay out of the water!"

He climbed up on to the tip of the fox's nose and, as they watched, the fox tossed him up in the air and caught him with a snap of his jaws. The gingerbread man was gone in one gulp.

"Well," said the old woman. "That's the last time I make one of those!"

The fox smiled. He knew that you had to be smart to catch a gingerbread man.

Snow-White and Rose-Red

Snow-White and Rose-Red

There was once a widow who lived in the forest with her two daughters in a cottage in the garden of which there grew two beautiful rose bushes. One bore white flowers and the other red. The two girls had been named after the rose bushes; Snow-White was fair-haired, Rose-Red was dark-haired and both were as pretty as the flowers after which they had been named.

The mother of Snow-White and Rose-Red was very proud of her daughters who helped to keep the cottage so clean and tidy. The mother had to work very hard to provide food for them all.

One winter's evening there came a loud banging on the cottage door.

When the mother opened the door, she saw a huge, brown bear standing there. She was very frightened but then the bear spoke gently,

"Please let me come in and get warm for a while. I am frozen."

So they let the bear sit by the fire. When he was warm, he got up to leave but they invited him to stay for the night and he accepted gratefully.

"Come whenever you like," said Snow-White and Rose-Red as he left the next morning so the bear came every night for the rest of the winter and the girls enjoyed his company.

When spring came, the bear said that he had to go away for the summer. The girls felt sad when they waved him off as they would miss him very much.

Some days later the girls were in the forest when they came upon a tiny dwarf, hopping angrily from foot to foot, with his beard caught in a crack in a tree trunk. The girls ran to help him.

"I suppose you have come to laugh at me," he snarled.

"Don't be silly!" said Snow-White. "We have come to help you."

No amount of pulling could free the dwarf's beard so, eventually, Snow-White took her scissors from her apron and cut off the end of it.

"Look what you have done to my beard!" the dwarf cried furiously. " A curse upon you!"

The dwarf had a bag of gold lying by him and he grabbed it and disappeared.

A little later, Snow-White and Rose-Red came upon the dwarf again. He was leaping up and down by the river with his beard tangled in his fishing line. They tried to free it but, finally, they had to use the scissors to cut off yet another bit.

The dwarf was free but angry and ungrateful.

"My beard! My pride and joy!" he cried. "Curses upon you!"

This time there was a bag of pearls beside him and he snatched it up and disappeared again.

One day, the girls saw a great hawk swooping towards earth. They heard a terrible scream and saw that the hawk had the struggling dwarf in its talons. The girls hit the hawk and, after pulling at the dwarf's coat, managed to free him. He fell to the ground in a heap, his face red with fury.

"Just look what you have done! I'm all battered and bruised and my lovely coat is torn."

The dwarf's rudeness was no surprise by now and the girls watched in silence as he picked up a bag containing jewels from the ground beside him and vanished from sight.

They were on their way home when they came across the dwarf once more. He had spread out all his treasures on the ground before him and Snow-White and Rose-Red gasped as the jewels sparkled in the sunshine but suddenly the dwarf saw them.

"What are you staring at?" he demanded angrily and began to gather up his treasures but he was stopped by a great roaring sound coming from the trees.

His fury turned to terror as a big, brown bear crashed through the undergrowth towards him. The dwarf panicked and there was no time to hide.

"Oh, Mr Bear, please forgive me!" he cried. "Spare my life, I beg you! I shall give you all these treasures! Look at these girls. They will make a you a tasty supper! Take them not me!"

But the bear gave a mighty sweep of his paw and the dwarf was killed in an instant.

Snow-White and Rose-Red, fearing for their own lives, ran away but the bear called them back.

"Snow-White and Rose Red, don't be afraid!"

The girls recognised their old friend and then saw that the bear's skin was falling away. In place of the bear stood a handsome man dressed in rich clothing.

"I am a king's son," he said. "That terrible dwarf stole all my treasures and changed me into a bear, condemning me to roam the forest until he died. Now he has been justly punished and I am free again."

The girls were delighted and went with the prince to tell their mother the good news.

The prince had never forgotten their kindness to him and in time he asked Snow-White to marry him and Rose-Red married his brother.

When the stolen treasures were recovered there was enough to ensure that they could live in wealth and comfort for the rest of their lives. The mother of Snow-White and Rose-Red went to live with them all and made sure she took with her the two precious rose bushes from her cottage garden.

The Princess and The Pea

The Princess and The Pea

Long ago, in a far distant kingdom there lived a king and queen and their son. He was their only child and, from the day he was born, they gave him the very best of everything. He grew up tall and strong, a credit to his parents, and was clever, good-natured and handsome.

The prince began to think that it was time he found a girl to love and to marry. Of course, there were many young ladies from noble families who would have dearly loved to have become the prince's wife, but the queen told her son,

"When you marry, you must marry a TRUE princess. No-one else will be good enough."

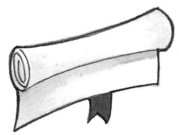

The prince told his mother he would only consider young ladies who came from other royal families but even this did not satisfy the queen.

"They may come from royal families," she said, "but they may still not be TRUE princesses."

"How shall I be able to tell which young lady is a TRUE princess?" the prince wanted to know.

"Trust me, my son. I shall find you a TRUE princess to marry," said his mother.

The queen sent out messengers to make it known that the prince was looking for a princess. Those who wanted to be considered were to tell the palace. Each would be invited in turn to spend a night in the palace's guest suite. The royal family would then decide on the prince's bride.

The announcement also stated that only TRUE princesses would be considered.

The queen then gathered her servants to prepare the guest suite. In the bedroom was a large, comfortable bed with a soft, feather mattress but the queen ordered the puzzled servants to bring in nineteen more mattresses and to pile them, one on top of another, on to the guest bed.

With twenty mattresses on it, the bed was so high that a ladder was needed for anybody trying to get into it! Then, when no-one was looking, the queen slipped a single pea underneath the mattress that lay at the very bottom of the pile.

For the next few weeks a carriage would arrive every day with another hopeful lady. All of them tried to convince the queen that they were suitable.

As all claimed to be of royal birth they were asked careful questions to make sure that they were telling the truth. After dinner, each princess was then shown to the guest suite.

Some were beautiful, some were charming and most of them really did come from royal families. The prince spent time with each and some he liked very much but, according to the queen, none of them was a TRUE princess. In the morning she would ask each one the same question,

"Did you sleep well last night?"

Each girl would reply politely,

"Yes thank you, Ma'am, I slept very well."

Then the queen would frown and when the girl had left, she would turn to her son and say,

"She was not a TRUE princess. We must continue looking."

The prince was puzzled. How could the queen tell that none of them was a TRUE princess?

As time passed, the number of princesses coming to see the prince grew smaller and smaller and it began to seem as if they would never find a TRUE princess. Weeks went by and the prince began to feel sure he would never marry but the queen told him not to worry.

"Your princess will come one day. Wait and see!"

One dark and stormy night, the prince was feeling very gloomy when there was a knock on the door of the palace. The prince followed the servant who opened the door and he saw a very bedraggled young woman standing there.

"I am so cold and wet," she said. "May I stay here for the night until the storm dies down?"

He led her to a fireside chair and gave her hot food and wine. As she drank he could see her clothes were threadbare and she was barefoot.

"I was found in a forest far from here by a poor woman," the girl said. "She brought me up and tells me I am a princess from a distant kingdom."

She was beautiful and charming and the prince, wondering if she could be a TRUE princess, went to tell the queen.

The queen looked doubtful but said that of course she could stay for the night. The prince showed the girl to the guest suite and said goodnight, leaving her to climb the ladder to the top of the pile of mattresses.

Next morning, at breakfast, the girl looked even more tired than before. When the queen asked if she had slept well she hesitated and said,

"I hate to be rude, Ma'am, but I cannot lie. The bed was so lumpy I could not sleep a wink!"

"My son! At last we have found a TRUE princess!" the queen said delightedly.

The prince too was delighted but also puzzled.

"How do you know she is a TRUE princess?"

His mother took them both to the guest suite and took out the pea from under the mattress.

"Only a TRUE princess could feel *this* under twenty feather mattresses," she said.

The prince and princess laughed at the queen's craftiness and when he asked her to marry him she agreed and they went to make preparations for a great wedding celebration.

Rumpelstiltskin

Rumpelstiltskin

Once there lived, in a certain kingdom, a poor miller who had a very beautiful daughter. She was, moreover, exceedingly shrewd and clever and the foolish miller was so proud of her that, one day, he told the king of the land that his daughter could spin gold out of straw.

Now this king was very fond of money and, when he heard the miller's boast, his avarice was excited and he ordered the girl to be brought before him. Then he led her to a chamber where there was a great quantity of straw, gave her a spinning-wheel and said,

"All this must be spun into gold before morning if you value your life."

It was in vain that the poor maiden declared that she could do no such thing: the chamber was locked and she remained alone.

She sat down and began to lament her hard fate when, suddenly, the door opened and a droll-looking, little man hobbled in and said,

"Good morrow to you, my lass. What are you weeping for?"

"Alas!" answered she. "I must spin this straw into gold for my life's sake and I know not how."

"What will you give me," asked the dwarf, "to do it for you?"

"My necklace," replied the maiden.

He took her at her word and set himself down at the wheel. Round it went merrily and presently the work was done and the gold all spun.

When the king came and saw this, he was greatly astonished and pleased but his heart grew still more greedy for gold and he shut up the poor miller's daughter again with more straw.

Again, she knew not what to do but, again, the little man opened the door and asked,

"What will you give me to do your task?"

"The ring on my finger," replied she.

So the little man took the ring and began to work at the wheel till, by morning, all was done.

The king was vastly delighted to see all this glittering treasure but still his greed was not satisfied and he took the miller's daughter into a yet larger room and said,

"All this must be spun tonight and, if you succeed, you shall be my queen."

As soon as she was alone the dwarf came in and said,

"What will you give me to spin gold for you this third time?"

"I have nothing left," said she.

"Then promise me," said the little man, "your first child when you are queen."

"That may never be," thought the miller's daughter but, as she knew no other way to get the task done, she promised him what he asked and soon the straw had again turned into gold.

At the birth of her first child the queen rejoiced very much and forgot the dwarf and her promise but, one day, he came into her chamber and reminded her of it.

Then she offered him all the treasures of the kingdom in exchange but, in vain. At last he said,

"I will give you three days and, if during that time you can tell me my name, you shall keep your child."

Now the queen lay awake all night thinking of all the odd names that she had ever heard and then sent messengers to enquire after new ones.

The next day she began with Timothy, Benjamin, Jeremiah and all the names she could remember but, to all, he said,

"That is not my name."

The second day she offered strange names Bandy-legs, Hunch-back, Crook-shanks and so on but the dwarf still said to every one of them,

"That is not my name."

On the third day one of the messengers came back and said,

"Yesterday, as I was climbing a high hill among the trees of the forest where the fox and the hare bid each other goodnight, I saw a little hut and before the hut burnt a fire and round about the fire danced a funny, little man who sang,

'Merrily the feast I'll make,
Today I'll brew, tomorrow bake.
Merrily I'll dance and sing,
For next day will a baby bring.
Little does my lady dream,
Rumpelstiltskin is my name!' "

When the queen heard this, she jumped for joy.
The dwarf came again the third day and he asked,
   "Now, lady, what is my name?"
   "Is it John?"
   "No!"
   "Is it Tom?"
   "No!"

"Can your name be Rumpelstiltskin?"

"Some witch told you that! Some witch told
you that!" cried the little man and dashed his right
foot in a rage so deep into the floor that he was
forced to take hold of it with both hands to pull it
out.

He ran from the palace and was never seen
again.

The Snow Queen

The Snow Queen

Once there was a wicked sorcerer who had made a magic mirror. In it everything, no matter how beautiful or good, looked ugly. The sorcerer showed it to the nasty little imps, his pupils, and they took the mirror everywhere. They even wanted to see how heaven would look in it.

As they flew, the mirror shook and shook until it slipped from their hands, breaking into a million pieces, some as small as a speck of dust. If a tiny grain were to get into a child's eye, everything that child saw would seem bad and if a piece reached a child's heart, that heart turned to ice!

Kay and Gerda lived opposite one another. They were very poor but each had a garden, with a rambler rose, where they often played.

One day Kay suddenly cried out,

"Oh, I've got something in my eye! Oh, my heart! Now it is in my heart!"

It was a splinter of the magic mirror and now poor Kay was quite changed. He saw everything twisted, his heart was frozen and he played alone.

While he was playing with his toboggan a white sledge appeared, drawn by a white horse. In it was a figure in white furs who told him to tie his toboggan to the sledge. He was scared but did so and the sledge sped off. When it stopped a beautiful lady stepped out - the Snow Queen. She kissed him lightly on the forehead, a kiss as cold as ice. Then she kissed him again.

Kay forgot the cold, Gerda and everyone else and was no longer afraid. The Snow Queen took him into her sledge and up they went in the air.

Oh, how bitterly little Gerda cried for Kay! Then spring came and the rose budded again.

"Kay is dead," Gerda told the swallows.

"We do not believe it," they twittered and, in the end, even Gerda could not think it was true.

"I will give you my new shoes if you will bring me to Kay," said Gerda to the river and, throwing her shoes into the water, she got into a boat which drifted away until at last it came to a strange, little house.

An old woman came out and Gerda told her about Kay. She took Gerda inside and gave her cherries to eat while she combed her hair with a magic comb to make her forget about Kay.

She wanted Gerda to stay as she had always wanted a little girl for her own. She charmed all the roses in the garden away in case they reminded Gerda of Kay. Sometimes Gerda thought she missed one particular flower but did not know which until she saw a rose painted on the old woman's hat and suddenly remembered Kay. She wept and where her tears fell a rose bush grew.

"He is not dead," the roses said.

"I must look for him," cried Gerda and set off without delay. Soon a big crow came and Gerda asked him if he had seen Kay.

"Perhaps, but surely he has forgotten you for the princess," said the crow and told of a princess who had promised to marry the man clever enough to make her laugh. All had failed till the arrival of a boy with a toboggan whose tales were wonderful and she had married him.

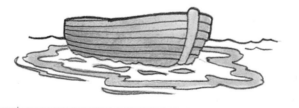

"Oh, will you take me there?" cried Gerda and the crow took her to a palace and showed her the princess's room. Gerda held her lamp and looked at the prince and called Kay's name. The prince awoke and sat up but it was not Kay. So she told her tale to the prince and princess and then fell asleep exhausted.

Next morning they gave Gerda fur-lined boots and a muff and a carriage to go and look for Kay. Gerda bade them farewell and the carriage rolled on through a forest until it was stopped by robbers. A woman drew out a big knife but, before she could hurt Gerda, her own daughter called out,

"She must play with me! She must give me her boots and her muff!"

That night Gerda stayed with the robbers. Wood-pigeons sat in the rafters above a reindeer tied to the wall. Gerda heard the pigeons coo,

"We have seen Kay. He was sitting in the sledge of the Snow Queen."

"Where did they go?" cried Gerda.

"To Finland," the pigeons said.

Next morning Gerda told the robber girl what the pigeons had said and she nodded and said,

"The reindeer will carry you to Finland."

Away it sped, running day and night. At last they reached Finland and stopped at a house. A woman let them in and they told her Kay's story.

"There is a splinter in Kay's heart," she said, "that must be removed or the Snow Queen will keep him for ever."

Kay had forgotten Gerda and his previous life and enjoyed living in the Snow Queen's castle but, when Gerda arrived, the Snow Queen was away and Kay was alone. Gerda knew him at once and kissed him and held him tight, crying,

"Kay, have I found you at last?"

Kay did not answer for his heart was frozen but then Gerda's tears fell on his chest and sank down into his heart and melted it. He recognised Gerda and burst into tears and his tears washed the speck of the magic mirror out of his eye.

"Gerda!" he cried. "At last!"

Gerda now wept for joy. Hand in hand they ran to the reindeer, waiting to take them home.

The roses were in bloom in the garden and Kay and Gerda knew they were really together again at last.

The Goose Girl

The Goose Girl

An old queen had a beautiful daughter who was betrothed to a prince living a long way off. When the time came for her marriage, the queen gave her a waiting-maid and each had a horse for the journey. The princess's was called Falada and could speak.

The old queen cut off a lock of her hair and gave it to her daughter saying,

"Take care of this for it is a charm which may be of use to you."

They said goodbye and the princess put the lock safely in her dress and set off. Later, as they were riding by a brook she said to her maid,

"Pray, fetch me some water in my golden cup out of the brook."

"No," said the maid. "If you are thirsty, get down and lie by the water and drink. I will not be your waiting-maid any longer."

The princess was so thirsty that she got down and drank. She wept and said,

"Alas! Alas! What will become of me?"

The lock of hair said,

"Alas! Alas! If your mother knew it
Sadly, sadly her heart would rue it!"

The princess was very meek so she said nothing but, later on, feeling thirsty again she said,

"Pray, fetch me some more water."

"I will not be your waiting-maid," said the girl even more haughtily than before.

The princess dismounted and lay down to drink but, as she did so, the lock of hair fell from her dress without her seeing it.

The maid, however, did see it and, knowing the princess would now be in her power, said,

"I shall ride Falada now."

The wicked maid forced the princess to give up her horse, take off her royal clothes and put on her own shabby ones. Near the end of the journey she even threatened to kill her mistress should she ever tell anyone what had happened. But Falada saw it all.

At the royal court, the prince ran to meet them and lifted the maid from her horse, thinking that she was his bride. They went inside and the true princess was told to wait in the courtyard.

The old king saw her and, as she looked too delicate for a waiting-maid, asked who she was.

"I brought her with me for company," said the false bride. "Pray, give her some work to do."

"I have a lad, called Curdken, who takes care of my geese," he said. "She may go to help him."

The false bride then said to the prince, as she was afraid that Falada would tell the truth,

"Tell one of your slaughterers to cut off my horse's head for it was very unruly on the road."

The prince ordered that the faithful Falada be killed and when the princess heard she begged the man to nail Falada's head above the gate so that she might see him as she passed. Next morning, at the gate she said sorrowfully,

"Falada, I see you hanging there!" and the head answered,

> *"Bride, fair Bride, you must beware.*
> *Alas! Alas! If your mother knew it*
> *Sadly, sadly her heart would rue it!"*

Curdken and the princess drove the geese to the meadow. She sat on a bank and let down her hair which was like pure gold. When Curdken saw it glitter, he ran to grab it but the princess cried,

"Blow, breezes, blow!
Let Curdken's hat go!
Blow, breezes, blow!
Let him after it go!
O'er hills, dales and rocks
Away be it whirl'd,
Till the golden locks
Are all comb'd and curl'd!"

A wind blew off Curdken's hat and he had to run after it. When he came back she had put her hair up. He was very sulky but they watched the geese until evening and then drove them home.

Next day, Falada spoke the same words to the princess. Then she and Curdken went to the meadow and again she sat down to comb her hair. When Curdken once more ran up to take hold of it the princess cried out the same words and the wind again blew off his hat and he had to chase it.

That evening, Curdken said to the old king,

"That strange girl teases me all day long."

The king made Curdken tell everything and then told him to go out as usual the next day. When morning came, the king hid by the gate and heard what the princess and Falada said and then hid behind a bush in the meadow to hear and see what would happen there. In the evening he asked the princess to explain her actions and she said,

"That I cannot do or I shall lose my life."

But the old king begged so hard that she told him all. He gave her some royal robes and called his son and told him everything. The prince rejoiced at finding his true princess and admired her beauty, meekness and patience. That evening, at dinner, the old king told the story as if it were one he had once heard, and asked the false bride what a just punishment would be for such a crime.

"She should be thrown into a cask stuck round with nails," she said. "Then two horses should drag it along the streets until she is dead."

"So be it," said the old king. "Since you have judged yourself, so shall it be done to you."

The prince was married to the true princess and they reigned over the kingdom in peace and happiness all their lives.

Jack and The Beanstalk

Jack and The Beanstalk

Long ago, in a tiny village, lived a boy called Jack. He and his mother were poor and one by one their animals died until there was only one old cow left.

"Jack, take the cow to market and sell her for a good price," said his mother. "She is too old to produce milk and we need the money for food."

Jack set off for market and met an old man resting by the road.

"On the way to market, are you?" he asked.

"Yes," said Jack. "I must sell my cow."

"I'll take the cow in exchange for these magic beans," said the man. "Plant them in your garden and amazing things will happen. You'll see!"

The magic beans sounded exciting so Jack gave the cow to the man and took the beans home.

"You stupid boy!" cried his mother tearfully. "These beans won't grow! Now we shall starve!"

She threw the beans out of the window and Jack went to bed hungry and unhappy.

Next morning he opened the door and gasped as he saw a huge beanstalk reaching up to the sky.

"I wonder how high this beanstalk goes," thought Jack and he began to climb.

All day long, Jack climbed. When he reached the top it was dark. A road stretched ahead of him and he followed it until he came to a huge castle. He knocked on the door and a woman answered.

"I'm tired and hungry," said Jack. "May I rest here and have some food?"

"You may have some food," said the woman, "but, when my husband, the giant, comes home, run for your life. He eats little boys like you."

The woman ushered him into a huge kitchen and he had a delicious meal. Suddenly he heard the thunder of giant footsteps and hid in a big copper pot. The giant came in and roared,

"Fee, fi, fo fum,
I smell the blood of an Englishman!"

"Nonsense, dear," insisted his wife. "Your hunger is making you imagine things."

He ate his meal noisily and then bellowed,

"Wife! Bring me my money!"

Jack carefully lifted the lid of the pot and saw the giant's wife stagger in, carrying several bags of gold. The giant emptied the gold on to the table and began to count it while his wife went to bed.

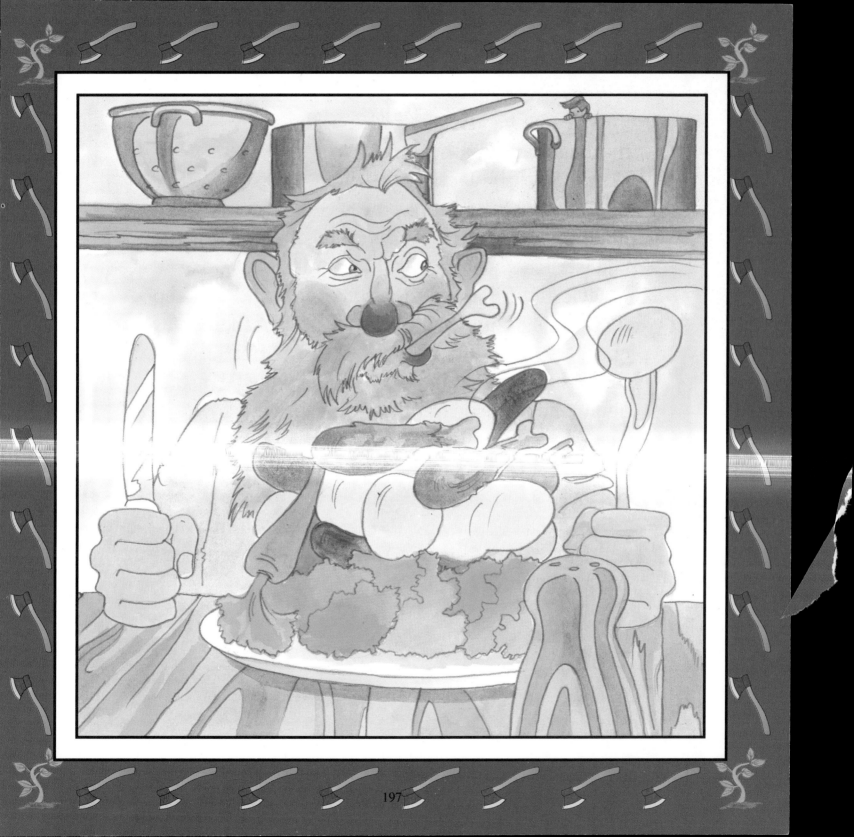

When he had finished, he put the coins back in the bags, laid his head on his arms and went to sleep. Silently, Jack climbed out of his pot, crept up to the table and took three bags of gold. Then he slipped out of the castle and back down the beanstalk.

Jack and his mother had enough gold to keep them living comfortably for the rest of their lives and Jack should have settled down but he was restless, so, one morning, he climbed the beanstalk again and headed straight for the castle where the giant's wife answered the door.

"You must not come in!" she cried. "My husband will find you and eat you for sure!"

But Jack looked so tired that she let him in for a meal. He had hardly finished eating when he heard the giant's roar and ran to hide.

"Fee, fi, fo fum,
  I smell the blood of an Englishman!"
"Don't be silly, dear," his wife spoke gently.
"It's only the sausages for supper you can smell."
    After eating his supper he called,
"Wife! Bring me my hen!"
    She brought it to him and bade him goodnight
and the giant roared at the hen,
"Lay, hen, lay!"
    The hen laid a shining, golden egg on the table
and carried on laying until there was a huge pile of
golden eggs. Then the giant dozed off to sleep.
    Jack sneaked up to the table, grabbed the hen,
holding her beak to keep her quiet, and ran out.
    When Jack reached home he gave the hen to
his mother. They would now be very wealthy.

Jack's mother was very afraid, however.

"Jack," she said. "One day your father went to market and never came back. A travelling man came and told me that they had found the giant's castle and the giant ate your father up. Jack, this must be the giant you have been stealing from! Please don't go back!"

But Jack would not listen and vowed to avenge his father's death.

The giant's wife was terrified when she saw him again but, at last, let him in although he had no time to eat before the giant returned.

"Fee, fi, fo fum,
   I smell the blood of an Englishman!"
She calmed the giant down again and gave him his dinner. When he had finished he bellowed,
   "Wife! Bring me my golden harp!"

"Play, harp, play!" the giant commanded.

With song after song the harp entertained the giant until he commanded it to stop. When he slept, Jack snatched the harp but it cried out,

"Help, master, help!" and the giant woke up.

"Fee, fi, fo fum!

I shall eat you. Come to me, come!"

Jack, carrying the screeching harp, ran to the beanstalk with the giant lumbering after him. Jack slithered to the bottom, ran indoors and grabbed his axe. He swung the axe and chopped at the beanstalk until it broke.

"That is for my father!" shouted Jack as the giant fell to the ground with a tremendous crash.

Jack's adventures were over and he and his mother had no need to fear the giant ever again.

Rapunzel

Rapunzel

Once there lived a poor craftsman and his wife who longed for a baby and after many years their dream came true. They were so poor that they often went hungry and, in desperation to feed his wife, the craftsman stole some vegetables from a nearby garden but the garden belonged to a wicked witch and she caught him. He begged for mercy.

"My wife is to have a baby," he said, "and she needs proper food!"

"You may take the vegetables and return to your wife but when the child is born it shall be mine," said the heartless witch.

The craftsman and his wife were very frightened.

When the baby was born they named her Rapunzel and tried to forget about the witch but, one night, the witch appeared, took the baby and disappeared. The craftsman and his wife never saw their beloved daughter again.

The witch kept Rapunzel all to herself in a tall tower in a lonely forest with the door blocked so that she could not escape. As she grew, the witch would never let her cut her hair and when she visited her would call up to the high window,

"Rapunzel, Rapunzel, let down your gold hair."

Then Rapunzel would let down her long hair and the witch would take hold of it and use it to climb up the tower and in through the window.

The witch brought her food and clothes but Rapunzel was often lonely and longed to be able to talk to someone and explore the world outside. She often sang songs that she had made up.

One day, a prince rode by and heard her sing.

"What a sad song! Who sings so sweetly?" he said and then heard a second, rasping voice say,

"Rapunzel, Rapunzel, let down your gold hair."

The prince saw a beautiful girl let down her long hair from the high window of the tower and watched as an ugly, old woman climbed up and in through the window. He waited till she climbed back down and vanished from sight in the forest. Then he walked to the tower and called out,

"Rapunzel, Rapunzel, let down your gold hair."

She was amazed to see him, and a little fearful, but the prince assured her that he meant her no harm. So Rapunzel let her hair down from the window and he climbed up. They talked for a long time and the prince soon realised that he had fallen in love with Rapunzel. He promised he would return as often as he could.

One day Rapunzel said to him,

"I cannot stay locked in this tower for ever. I need your help to escape."

He gladly agreed to help and the next evening brought a skein of strong silk thread. Rapunzel began to weave a ladder to escape from the tower and every evening the prince brought more silk.

Rapunzel worked on her ladder but kept it well hidden from the witch. One day, however, the witch did not come at her usual time and, when she called to Rapunzel, the girl thought it was the prince. She let her hair down calling,

"Hurry, my darling. I have been so lonely!"

The witch was furious and demanded to know whom Rapunzel had been seeing. Rapunzel, although terrified, would not say, so the witch flew into a rage, picked up a pair of scissors and cut off all Rapunzel's beautiful hair.

Then she cast a spell to banish Rapunzel from the tower and sent her far away into a wilderness to wander for ever, lost and alone.

The witch waited in the tower until the prince returned, calling out,

"Rapunzel, Rapunzel, let down your hair."

The witch dangled Rapunzel's hair out of the window and when the prince reached the sill he found the furious witch awaiting him.

"So you think you can take Rapunzel away from me, do you," she screamed. "I am too clever for you! Rapunzel has gone for ever!"

The witch pushed the prince from the window-sill with a mighty heave. He fell to the ground, landing in a thorn bush. The thorns scratched his eyes, blinding him, and he staggered away into the forest, unable to see but too sorrowful to care.

The prince wandered many miles in search of Rapunzel, calling her name continually.

Many months later the prince reached the wilderness where the witch had sent Rapunzel. He was still calling her name but he was beginning to fear he would never find her.

Suddenly a voice cried out,

"Who is calling me? I am here."

"Rapunzel! Have I found you at last?" he whispered joyfully as he turned towards her.

"Yes, my darling prince! You have found me!" and Rapunzel ran towards him, weeping with joy.

As she kissed the prince, Rapunzel's tears fell into his eyes and he found he could see again.

Rapunzel and the prince returned to his kingdom where they lived happily ever after.

The Emperor's New Clothes

The Emperor's New Clothes

A long time ago in a country far away, there ruled an emperor. He was very vain and loved to parade in front of his people at the head of grand processions, magnificently dressed in regal robes.

All the tailors in the country vied with each other to be allowed to make clothes for him.

One day two men arrived at the palace, told the guards they were tailors and asked to see the emperor. He agreed to see them and was amazed at what they said.

"Your Majesty, we wish to make you superb robes from a special cloth. We will weave this cloth on our own looms and it has magic powers.

"A wise person will be able to see the magnificent cloth but a fool will see nothing. We have chosen you to be the first to wear this cloth for you are the most elegant man in the land."

The emperor was delighted. He gave the men a bag of gold and told them to start work at once. The two rascals set up their looms in a room in the palace. They gave orders for the finest gold and silver threads to be be brought but they did not use this thread. They packed it away in sacks to sell for a good price in the market and just pretended to work on the empty looms. As they left the palace that evening, they told the guards that the cloth was half-finished.

The next day they returned and pretended to be working on the empty looms once more.

The emperor had promised them that he would not look at the cloth before it was finished but, unable to contain his curiosity, he sent his man-servant to visit them at their work. He knew that the magic cloth was invisible to fools but was sure he would be wise enough to see it. However, when he went in he could only see the men working at what appeared to be empty looms.

"I cannot see the magic cloth, but how can I admit that to the emperor? I will lose my job," he thought and decided he would have to pretend.

"What do you think of our cloth?" they asked.

"Beautiful!" he replied. "How ever can I describe such amazing cloth to the emperor?"

"Describe it this way," the rascal grinned and gave him a long description of exotic cloth.

The emperor was even more excited after his manservant told him about the cloth and could hardly wait for it to be finished. Finally, the tailors came to say that they had completed the weaving and wanted him to see the cloth before they made it into robes so he went to the work-room and stared at the empty looms in dismay.

"I cannot see the magic cloth but if my people find out that I am a fool they will no longer have me as emperor so I will have to pretend," he thought to himself and said aloud to the tailors,

"This is the most beautiful cloth ever seen."

He ordered them to make the cloth into robes for him to wear in a grand, royal procession and the two rascals grinned to themselves while they pretended to work day and night on the robes.

On the morning of the great procession, the tailors went to the emperor and held up their hands as if they were holding up clothes for inspection.

"Our great work is complete, Your Majesty!" they announced. "We hope you are satisfied!"

The courtiers could see nothing at all but they pretended they could and agreed that the clothes were the most beautiful there had ever been.

"You are the most skilful of tailors," said the delighted emperor. "I shall reward you handsomely," he added as he went to his chambers where the tailors pretended to dress him in his new clothes.

Trying not to shiver with the cold, he stared into his mirror but, try as he could, he could see no clothes, just his own plump, pink body.

The rascally tailors were enjoying themselves. "Isn't the robe perfection itself?" they said.

"It is quite the finest outfit I have ever worn," said the emperor but, secretly, he wished he were clever enough to see the clothes.

Soon the great procession set off. Everybody had come to see the new magic robes and, as the emperor went by, everyone thought the same thing.

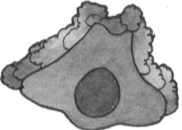

"If I cannot see the clothes, I must be a fool!"

So, just as the emperor, his manservant and all the courtiers had done, they decided to pretend, for none of them wanted to be thought foolish.

"Look at the colours! Look at the style!"

The emperor's chest swelled with pride as he heard all the praise. It was so nice to be admired.

The procession passed by a young boy who had not been told about the magic robes. He took one look at the emperor and burst out laughing.

"The emperor has no clothes on!" he shouted and, all around, the people began to whisper,

"The boy is right! The emperor *is* naked!"

The boy had given people the courage to tell the truth and the emperor had heard the boy too. He blushed with embarrassment and realised that he was indeed naked and that he *was* a fool.

Somewhere far away, the two wily tailors were laughing at the foolish emperor and discussing how to spend the fortune they had made.

Meanwhile, the emperor returned as quickly as possible to the palace, cold and ashamed but much wiser. Never again would he let his vanity stop him from using his common sense.

The Musicians of Bremen

The Musicians of Bremen

In a small village, near a town called Bremen, lived an old donkey. He deserved a happy retirement but, knowing his master had no more use for him, he broke his tethering rope and left.

"I have always done as my master wished but now I want to go to Bremen and be a musician," he said and made his way down the high road where he met an old dog panting by the roadside.

"You look tired. Have you far to go?"

"I don't know," the dog sighed. "My master has no more use for me as I'm too old so I ran away."

"I'm going to Bremen to become a musician. Why don't you come too?" asked the donkey.

They set off and soon came across a cat.

"I used to hunt rats for a farmer," she said, "but I'm too slow to catch them now so I left."

"All cats can sing," said the dog. "I listen to them all night. Why not sing with our band?"

The cat agreed and the three animals walked on. Soon they saw a cockerel sitting on a wall.

"Nobody likes my singing any more," said the cockerel sadly, "so I've no home now."

The others welcomed him to the band and they went on along the road to Bremen. By now it was growing dark and they needed to find somewhere to sleep so they went into a small wood where the cockerel spotted a light amongst the trees.

"Maybe there's a house there," he said. "Let's take a look. They might have some food there."

Soon the animals came to a cottage. There was a lot of noise and laughter coming from inside. The donkey sidled up to a window and looked in.

"Robbers!" he whispered. "They're having a party! There's enough food on the table to feed a hundred people and piles of gold and jewels!"

"Lots of food and a place to stay the night; it would be lovely!" said the dog. "Can we get in?"

"I think I may have an idea," said the cat with a wink. "This is what we will do ..."

As instructed, the animals piled themselves one on top of the other. First the donkey, then the dog, then the cat, with the cockerel on top. They wobbled up to the window and burst into the loudest song they could sing. The noise was appalling - braying, barking, yowling, crowing.

The robbers were terrified. The animals kept up the noise as they smashed their way in through the window.

"Aaah! Monsters!" yelled the robbers, rushing to get out, too scared to see what was happening.

The four animals ate well that night and then got ready to sleep. The donkey found a pile of dry straw to lie on in the courtyard: the dog snuggled down on an old cushion behind the front door: the cat settled on the rug in front of the fire: the cockerel perched on the mantelpiece and they were all so tired that they soon fell asleep.

Meanwhile the robbers were talking in the woods and felt they had been foolish to run away so fast and leave all their booty behind.

"We don't even know what it was that scared us!" said one. "It might have gone away by now."

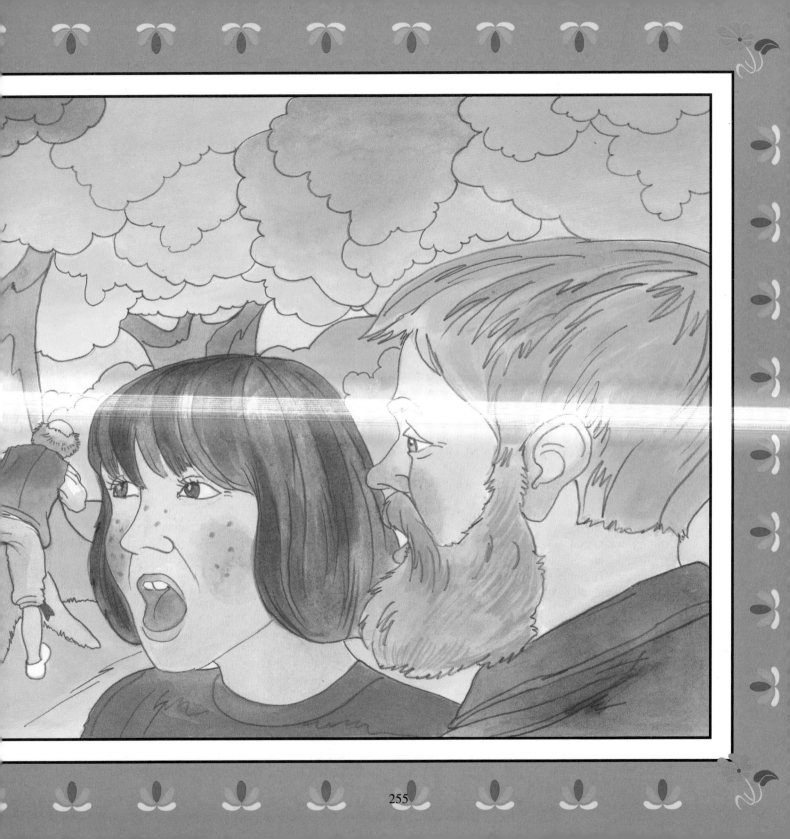

"One of us should go back and see," said another and they ordered the youngest to go.

Nervously, the youngest robber crept through the trees to the cottage. He opened the back door and peered into the darkness. He felt his way carefully into the living room, trying to be quiet. Suddenly he tripped over a chair leg. The sound of his stumble awoke the cat who opened her eyes. The dog woke as well but lay quietly listening.

The robber caught sight of the cat's eyes glowing in the hearth and thought they were the embers of the fire.

"If I light a match on these embers, I will be able to see better," he thought and, finding a match in his pocket, he tiptoed to the fireplace and stuck the match in the cat's eye ...

The cat hissed and clawed at him. Then the cockerel flapped past, beating his wings against his face. The robber screamed and stumbled past the front door where the dog sank his teeth into his leg. The robber screamed in pain and staggered outside where the donkey gave him an almighty kick. Moaning in pain and trembling with fear, the youngest robber limped back to his friends.

The cockerel flew up to the cottage roof.

"COCK-A-DOODLE-DOO!" he crowed gleefully.

The limping robber told a strange tale.

"The house is full of monsters!" he gasped. "We can never go back! A demon witch gouged at me with her talons! When I fought to get free, a winged phantom flew past me and beat me with its wings!" The robber's voice shook as he went on,

"Then a black monster plunged a knife into my leg! Another monster in the yard hit me so hard with two cudgels that I was sent flying and then I heard a voice from on high calling 'DOOM WILL COME TO YOU!' "

None of the robbers dared to return to collect their stolen booty, and, what was more, none dared to steal again. Every time they felt tempted, the youngest reminded them of the voice crying 'DOOM WILL COME TO YOU!' and they changed their minds. Crime did not pay, they decided.

As for the animals, they settled in the cottage where they spent a long and comfortable retirement. They never did go to Bremen and forgot all about becoming musicians but it did not matter. They had had a great adventure together and now they had as happy a life as anyone could wish for.

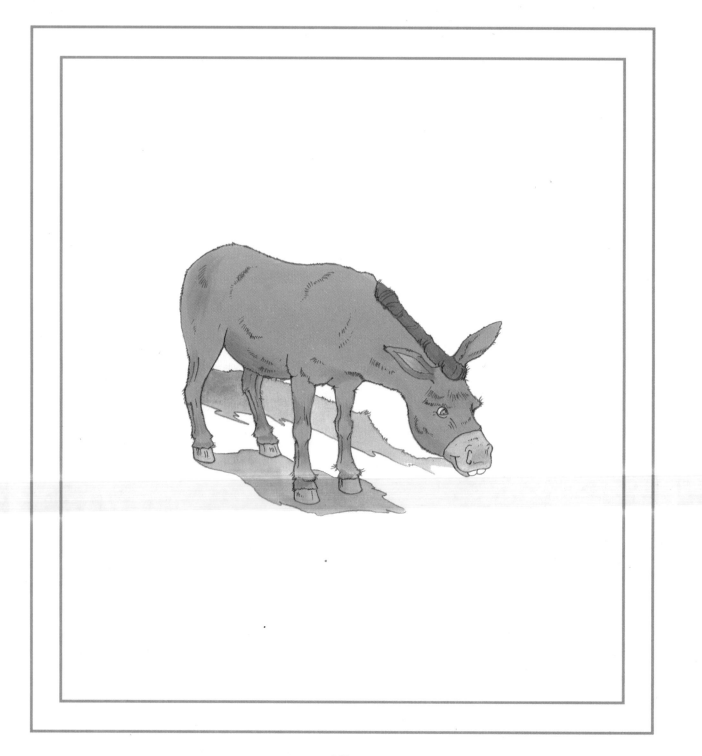

The Shepherdess and The Chimney-Sweep

The Shepherdess and The Chimney-Sweep

An old-fashioned, oak cabinet once stood in a parlour. It was carved from top to bottom and in the centre panel the carving was of a man. He was a ridiculous figure with crooked legs and small horns. The children who lived in the house called him the 'crooked-legged Field-Marshal-Major-General-Corporal-Sergeant'.

His eyes were always fixed upon the table where a pretty, little, porcelain shepherdess stood. She was charming! Close by her stood a porcelain chimney-sweep with a ladder in his hand. They had been placed together and had become sweethearts.

Not far off stood a porcelain figure three times as large as the others. It was an old, Chinese mandarin who could nod his head. He had declared he was the grandfather of the shepherdess and so, when the 'crooked-legged Field-Marshal-Major-General-Corporal-Sergeant' proposed to the shepherdess, he nodded his head in consent.

"You will have a husband who, I truly believe, is of mahogany wood," said the old mandarin. "He has a whole cabinet full of silver, besides a store of no-one knows what in the secret drawers."

"I will not live in that dismal cabinet," declared the little shepherdess. "I have heard that eleven porcelain ladies are already imprisoned there."

"Then you shall be the twelfth," rejoined the mandarin. "Tonight you shall be married!"

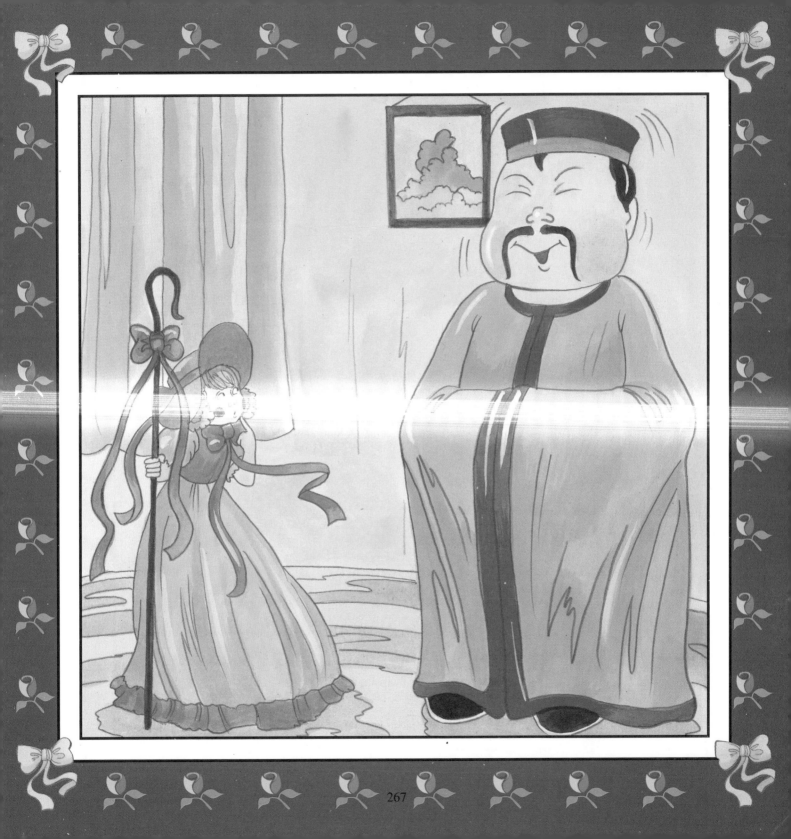

Then he fell asleep. The little shepherdess wept and turned to her beloved chimney-sweep.

"I believe I must ask you," said she, "to take me into the wide world, for here I cannot stay."

"I will do whatever you wish and I think I can support you by my work, so, let us go now," he replied and he showed her how to climb down the gilded foliage twining round the leg of the table.

The two of them had just reached the floor when the 'crooked-legged Field-Marshal-Major-General-Corporal-Sergeant' shouted,

"Look, they are eloping!"

They were frightened when they saw that the mandarin had awoken and was rocking to and fro with rage.

"The mandarin is coming!" she cried.

"Suppose we creep into the large pot-pourri vase in the corner," said the chimney-sweep. "There we can rest upon roses and lavender."

"That will not do at all," said she, "for the old mandarin was once betrothed to the pot-pourri vase and, no doubt, there is still some slight friendship existing between them. No, we must go into the wide world."

"Have you thought how large it is and that we may never return home?" he asked.

"I have," she replied and he said,

"My path leads through the chimney. Have you the courage to creep with me through the stove, the flues and the tunnel? At the top there is a cavern that leads into the world."

Then he led her to the door of the stove and she followed him through the pitch-dark tunnels.

"Now we are in the chimney," said he, "and look what a lovely star shines above us!"

And there was a star in the sky, shining as if to light the way. They crawled and crept - so very high - but he guided her, and showed her the best places to put her tiny, porcelain feet, till they reached the edge of the chimney and could rest.

Heaven, with all its stars, was above them; the town, with all its roofs, lay beneath them; the wide, wide world surrounded them. The shepherdess had never imagined all this and she leant her head on his arm and wept bitterly.

"The world is too large!" she exclaimed. "I shall never be happy until I am once more upon my little table! I have followed you into the wide world, surely you can follow me home again, if you love me!"

He talked very sensibly to her, reminding her about the old, Chinese mandarin and her fear of the ugly 'crooked-legged Field-Marshal-Major-General-Corporal-Sergeant' but she wept so hard and kissed him so fondly that, at last, he could not but yield to her request, unreasonable as it was.

So they crawled back down the chimney and found themselves once more in the dark stove.

They listened from behind the door. Everything was quite still. They peeped out. Alas! On the ground lay the old mandarin for, in trying to follow the runaways, he had fallen off the table and broken into three pieces. His head lay in a corner.

"Oh no! How shocking!" she exclaimed. "Grandfather is in pieces and we are the cause!"

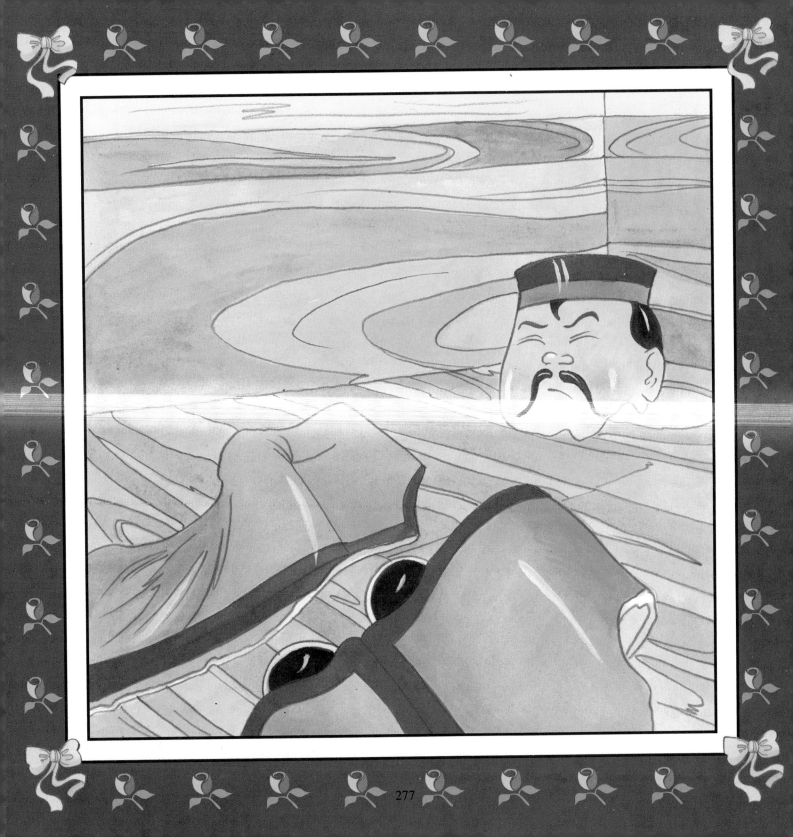

"He can be put back together," said the chimney-sweep. "If they glue his back and put a rivet in his neck, he will be as good as new."

They climbed back on the table. The old mandarin was put back together again. He was as good as new but could no longer nod his head.

"You have grown very proud since you broke," said the 'crooked-legged Field-Marshal-Major-General-Corporal-Sergeant', "but I do not see that there is anything to be proud of. Am I to have her or not?"

The couple gazed imploringly at the old mandarin. They were afraid lest he should nod his head but, nod he could not, and, as he did not wish to admit he had a rivet in his neck, he said nothing. So the shepherdess and the chimney-sweep remained together and loved each other for ever.

THE END